A TEMPLAR BOOK

Produced by The Templar Company plc,
Pippbrook Mill, London Road, Dorking, Surrey RH4 1JE, Great Britain.

Text copyright © *The Wishing Hat* 1950 by Darrell Waters Limited
Illustration and design copyright © 1994 by The Templar Company plc
Enid Blyton is a registered trademark of Darrell Waters Limited

This edition produced for Parragon Books,
Unit 13-17, Avonbridge Trading Estate, Atlantic Road, Avonmouth, Bristol BS11 9Q

This book contains material first published as
The Wizard's Hat in The Astonishing Ladder
First published by Macmillan 1950

Illustrated by Sophie Allsopp

Printed and bound in Italy

ISBN 1 85813 657 1

Enid Blyton's

POCKET LIBRARY

THE WISHING HAT

Illustrated by Sophie Allsopp

·PARRAGON·

Spillikins the Pixie went into
Dame Twinkle's teashop for
tea. He took off his pointed
cap and hung it up on a
hook behind his chair.
Then he ordered tea.

He looked round the shop. There were quite a lot of people there. He saw See-Saw the Wizard, eating sardines on gingerbread, a meal he liked very much. He saw Whistler the gnome drinking pink lemonade. And in the corner were Flip and Flap, the goblins, eating egg pie as fast as they could.

Spillikins was in rather a hurry so he asked for a glass of cold milk and a bun. He knew they wouldn't take very long to prepare. He munched his bun, and when it was finished he drank his milk down to the last drop. Then he paid his bill, took his cap off the hook, popped it on his head, and off he went.

It was a bright and beautiful sunny day, and Spillikins whistled cheerily as he thought of the day ahead.

He was going to see his friend Tippy, who lived in a lovely little cottage all by himself. Spillikins was going to help him to weed his garden. Tippy lived a long way away, and Spillikins soon got hot walking along in the sunshine that streamed over the fields.

"I wish somebody would wheel me in a barrow all the way there," he said to himself. "I'm getting jolly hot."

Just as he said that he heard something trundling behind him. He turned round – and what a funny thing! There was a big green wheelbarrow being pushed by an imp. He knocked Spillikins into the barrow and began to wheel him along.

"Ooh!" said Spillikins, in the greatest surprise. "He must have heard what I said, and decided to give me a ride. Well, this is better than walking."

The imp pushed him along, over the field and down the lanes.

Spillikins liked it – but the barrow was very hard to sit in, especially when it bumped over stones.

"I do wish I had a nice cushion or something to sit on," he said. "I'm getting quite bruised."

No sooner had he said the words than to his enormous surprise a huge yellow cushion appeared under him in the barrow! It was so soft and comfortable. Spillikins stared at it in amazement.

"Well, where did *you* come from?" he asked. "Hi, imp! Did you put this cushion here?"

But the imp said nothing. He just went on wheeling the barrow. Spillikins looked puzzled. There was something funny about the imp and the sudden way he had appeared.

"I am hot!" sighed the pixie, as the sun poured down hotter than ever. "I wish it would rain lemonade. How nice it would…"

He stopped suddenly. A great yellow cloud had blown over the sun, and large yellow drops of rain had started to fall all around.

"Buttons and buttercups!" cried Spillikins in astonishment, "I do believe it *is* raining lemonade. Ooh, what a funny thing!"

He opened his mouth and let the drops fall on to his tongue. They were delicious. Real, sweet lemonade, the nicest he had ever tasted. But after a while Spillikins began to feel rather wet, for the lemonade shower was a heavy one.

"I wish it would stop," he said. "I'm getting wet through."

In a trice the lemonade rain stopped and the sky became blue again. Spillikins looked very thoughtful. It was turning into a very strange day indeed.

"It seems to me as if all my wishes are coming true," he said. "I wonder why. Well, I'll wish a few more and see if they come true, too."

He thought for a moment. Then he wished.

"I wish I had a carriage made of gold, drawn by three giraffes," he said.

Immediately
a shining carriage stood
before him, and in front were
three tall giraffes! Spillikins was
delighted. He jumped out of the
wheelbarrow and ran to the carriage.

"I wish for a lion to drive my carriage and two kangaroos for footmen," he said.

Immediately, the wish came true. A lion sat on the box, dressed in a wonderful coachman's uniform, and two kangaroos dressed as footmen stood up behind.

"Now I wish for a suit of gold and a cloak of silver," said Spillikins. "Ha! Here they are! Don't I look grand!"

He got into the carriage, and told the lion to drive to his friend Tippy's house. He wished for all sorts of animals to follow him, all dressed in silver tunics and each carrying a present for his friend, and to his great delight they appeared, looking very grand indeed. There was an elephant, a camel with a present between his humps, a big furry panda and even an ostrich!

"That will make Tippy stare," thought Spillikins in delight. "He's always boasting about this, that and the other – but he won't boast any more when he sees *me*! Ha, and I've only got to wish and I can have anything I want!"

He was so excited that he could hardly wait to get to Tippy's. When at last the giraffe coach drew up outside his friend's cottage, he saw Tippy in the garden. But as soon as

Tippy saw the lion coachman, the giraffes, and the kangaroo footmen, he dropped his spade and fled indoors, frightened out of his life!

"Hi, Tippy! Tippy! Don't be afraid!" cried Spillikins. "It's only me! All my wishes are coming true!"

He ran indoors after Tippy and told him everything that had happened, and at last his friend believed him. He kept staring and staring at Spillikins in his gold tunic and silver cloak, and he wondered how it was that the pixie had managed to make his wishes come true.

"I don't know *how* it is," said Spillikins. "I really don't. It must just be some wonderful magic that has grown in me."

"Take off your hat and sit down," said Tippy. "You have had such a busy day. And besides, we don't need to do any weeding. We can just wish all the weeds away, and our work will be done. Ha, ha!"

"Ha, ha!" said Spillikins, and he pulled off his pointed cap.

"I say!" he said, staring at it. "This cap isn't mine! I must have taken the wrong one at the teashop. No wonder it felt so tight! It doesn't fit me at all well, and has given me quite a headache. I wish I had my own cap instead."

Whooooooosh! Almost before he had finished speaking, the cap he was holding flew away suddenly and another cap fell into Spillikins' hands. It was his own! But oh dear me, at the very same moment away went his silver cloak and gold tunic, leaving him in his plain old clothes. Off galloped the giraffe coach, and after it went all the animals with the presents Spillikins had brought for Tippy!

"Oh my, what's happening?"
cried Spillikins, all of a tremble.
"Hi! I wish you all to come back."
    But alas! they didn't come back.
They had gone for good!

"Oh dear, dear, dear!" sobbed Spillikins in the greatest disappointment. "I know what's happened. I must have taken Wizard See-Saw's hat by mistake, when I left the teashop. It was a wishing-cap – and that's why all the wishes I wished came true. Now I've got my own cap back I've lost the wishing power!"

"Oh!" groaned Tippy, getting up, "and to think we might have wished

all those weeds away! Why didn't we when we had the chance! Come along out, Spilly, and do some work."

Out they went, two very sad little pixies. That night they both dreamed of lions, kangaroos and giraffes – and I don't wonder at it, do you?